For David, Megan, and Mary

Copyright © 1995 by John Prater

First U.S. edition 1995

Library of Congress Cataloging-in-Publication Data

Prater, John.
The greatest show on earth / John Prater.—1st U.S. ed.
Summary: Young Harry feels useless because he lacks the talents
that other family members have as circus performers.
ISBN 1-56402-563-2
[1. Circus—Fiction. 2. Self-esteem—Fiction.] I. Title.
PZ7.P8867Gr   1995
[E]—dc20   94-24991

2 4 6 8 10 9 7 5 3 1

Printed in Belgium

The pictures in this book were done in pencil and watercolor.

Candlewick Press
2067 Massachusetts Avenue
Cambridge, Massachusetts 02140

THE GREATEST SHOW
ON EARTH

JOHN PRATER

Ladies and gentlemen, boys and girls, welcome to the circus!
It's the greatest show on earth.
There's magic and daring, amazing acts and incredible tricks . . .

and there's Harry. That's me!

This is Mom and Dad, who fly on the high trapeze.

And this is me . . . Oops!

This is my brilliant sister Sue. She can juggle almost anything.

And this is me . . . Ouch!

This is Wobble and Wilt—the cleverest acrobats you've ever seen.

And this is me . . . Whoops!

Abracadabra! This is Mr. Mysterio, conjuring flowers and fireworks from his hat.

And this is me . . . Bang!

This is Grandad on his wild whizzing wheels.

And this is me . . . Oooer! Yikes!

This is Grandma, who's so strong she can lift a trailer with one hand.

And this is me . . . Oh, dear!

And this is Wellington the dog. He tops the bill with his amazing balancing act. I can't fly through the air or juggle or balance or do magic tricks, so I take care of Wellington.

This is me.

Tonight's the night of the big show.
Ladies and gentlemen, boys and girls, silence, please,
for Wellington's amazing balancing act!

But Wellington has seen a mouse and . . . *WOOF! SQUEAK!* Oh, no!

CLATTER! WHOOSH! Help!

BOING! WHEE! I'm flying!

SWOOSH! SWING! This is fun!

WOBBLE! WHIZZ! I can do it! Hooray!

Hooray for Mom and Dad the fliers, my sister Sue the juggler, Wobble and Wilt the acrobats, Mr. Mysterio the magician, Grandad the unicyclist, Grandma the strongwoman, my dog Wellington who walks the wire . . . and who else?

Let's hear it now! As loud as you can!
HOORAY FOR HARRY THE CLOWN!
That's me!